AF316933

CORIANDER, MEANDERING SLANDERER

CORIANDER, MEANDERING SLANDERER

LUKE CHANDLER

Бþ

PALESTRINIAC PRESS

Lake Zurich, IL

CORIANDER, MEANDERING SLANDERER

Published in the United States by Palestriniac Press.

Library of Congress Control Number: 2023908199

ISBN 979-8-218-17445-3

First Printing, 2023

10 9 8 7 6 5 4 3 2 1

For everyone everywhere,

And a few others as well

Contents

PROLOGUE

Your shoes, sir, are lacking,
Quite lacking, in blacking.
Need you spatterdashes? These
Hark from haberdasheries!
Yes, from two locations
To support two vocations
That differ only slightly
As one works only nightly;
Each got nine dollars cash
As they both haberdash.

I myself wouldn't dare;
It would mess up my hair
And leave ringing my ears
With the silence (save shears
And some pokings of needles with thread, and unwhirling
Of spools, and some flapping of ribbons unfurling).

Yes, my hair—I digress; but the blacking's ruled out
As it's lacking in all the locales thereabout
On account of the strike in thirteen local chapters
Of the Shoe Polish Psycholectronic Adapters.
Oh you know, all those unionized alchemisticians
Who by shoe-polish skills became fine electricians
Till the lighting-bolt forge sadly shut down for good
(Ah! such matters are so often misunderstood.)
And the spatterdash-haberdash industry boomed;
And in shoe polish tins was he thereby entombed.

Who, you ask? Why, old Narpner McMickmac-
 MacSchnauppold,
Who uncorked the fine wine that he tipped till he toppled;
That former First Foreman, most manic, but kind,
Who regrettably put in a state of rewind—
In a state of, that is to say, real regression—
His shoe-blacking factory. That's no confession,
For everyone knows, as it is common knowledge,
That McMickmac-MacSchnauppold did not go to college,
To say nothing of maj'ring in Neurobunglotics,
That discipline dealing with, sans the narcotics,
Brain-based electrical-chemical tracking
Resulting in conjured-up shiny shoe blacking.

Though no academic was he, nor a tradesman,
Kind Narp, dipsomaniac, was a third-baseman
Of the league that the Psycholectronic Adapters
Had founded among those thirteen local chapters.
Serendipitously did he die just last year
Amidst shoe polish tins and old bottles of beer,
Both empty: the latter, from drink he abused;
The former, alas! because never produced.
So the less ignominious tins, then, I heard,
Were used to surround him when he was interred.

But, again, I digress more egregiously still,
For I mean you no feelings of will that are ill:
Let us now disregard lacking blacking of shoe
And find out if the spatterdash look is for you!

CHAPTER 1

DINK rode his unicycle with his headphones on and dark sunglasses for good measure. He was in the process of circling the neighborhood block thrice, as was his custom, when he found himself on the windshield of a 1993 Ford Taurus that had been outfitted the prior year with an after-market red leather interior. *What a laugh,* thought Dink, *that now I have made the exterior red as well!* But he exaggerated, as it was only his broken nose that was bleeding, and the tan vehicle already had a red presence to passers-by on account of its bold carmine pinstripes. And caught on the back bumper, curiously, were a pair of baggy jeans, which dragged on the street.

The woman who stepped out of the car was six-foot-eight and wore platform shoes.

The goggles she wore were mirrored, had black leather buckles and, somehow, copper exhaust pipes, fulfilling the steampunk aesthetic perfectly. Upon closer inspection, Dink realized that she was not in fact a redhead like she first appeared but rather a brunette who wore an aluminum skullcap outfitted with some 10,000 implanted bits of copper wire, at varied lengths of 18 to 24 inches. The darkness of her eyebrows, eyelashes, and fine forearm hair betrayed her Visigothic ancestry. Dink was flabbergasted.

"Oh dark giantess, what is thy bidding?" whispered Dink, reverently.

"I am called Vleffix, but my friends call me Quirff, which I appreciate, as it preserves the unique double-F spelling of my Christian name. Now get in the car."

Quirff, as I shall call her (as she is not unlike someone who could very well be the dear friend of a loved one) courteously opened the door for Dink. The young man, freshly concussed, stumbled into the car and promptly vomited.

"Good . . . good," murmured your loved one's hypothetical boon companion, knowingly, as if to herself, though well within hearing range of our hurling hero.

The pungent sick simmered and smoked, corroding a hole clear through the floorboard.

"Hah! I saw you chugging that battery acid this morning. I just saved your life. Now get the rest of your arms and legs inside the vehicle, close the door, and start running."

Stunningly, the plan worked.

Dink Flapple ran as hard and as fast as he could to propel the vehicle, in Barney Rubble fashion, although in truth the old Ford never exceeded 2 miles an hour. Quirff only laughed as she took her Clinton-era ride out of neutral, putting it in park, and proceeded to remove her bionic left leg in a shower of sparks. Nay, it was her right—just as it was Dink's to scream a primal scream from the ensuing chaos. He was just about to, too, having inhaled the cabin's peculiar air for over three seconds straight in preparation for what would have been among the most apocalyptic of yawps. But before he could—

"Relax, O man of the age. Draw in your feet, and I shall make the pavement itself move as our means of transport."

Quirff casually handed Dink a half-finished Mr. Goodbar and a warm but unopened can of New Coke.

"Heh heh! Did that come with your ride?" quipped Dink nervously.

"Well, yes—yes, it was an original fixture, Mr. Flapple. . . ." she replied, with no small amount of embarrassment. Vleffix, whom we endearingly regard as Quirff, always became polite when she was feeling humiliated.

"Oh," remarked Dink, awkwardly. He thought it best to change the subject. "—You know, I'm deathly allergic to peanuts."

"And?"

"Well, you just handed me the peanuttiest candy bar there is."

"*That* is up for debate. Regardless, it's half-eaten. At best, it will make you half-dead."

"Why do you say 'at best'?"

"It's all part of the plan, battery acid hurler," she said with condescension.

And with that she duct-taped his mouth open, gently set the remains of the nutty treat squarely on his tongue, and waited for the enzymes in his saliva to break them down into sheer toxicity. Dink unhappily acquiesced, resigning himself to his certain half-death, and swallowed down what was now no more than a mealy sludge. She promptly untaped him, and he was not reticent to speak.

"Shall I be a zombie?"

"Hah! You wish!"

Before Dink could rebut Quirff's rather juvenile diss, his body dissed him—by way of multiple organ failure!

Vleffix (for she is no longer any friend of mine, if ever she had been) laughed uncontrollably at Flapple's hardship, but seemed to have made the fatal error of forgetting her own words: that he would not die but by half, as the Mr. Goodbar, being among her own guilty pleasures, was not left wholly unconsumed upon his initial encounter with her late twentieth-century vehicle. That, and Dink's guinea pig, Klaus, awoke from beneath his beanie and began stirring, to the steampunk mistress's abject horror.

"No! No! How his brains do melt and writhe most repulsively! Oh Dink, Dink!"

(Unbeknownst to all, the once-ingested battery acid—Dink imbibed it on a dare, figuring it was nothing more than electric eel urine—had cauterized the lining of Dink's stomach, effectively sealing it and removing from it all absorptive properties, thenceforth immunizing the misguided chap from anything and everything entering the body. But what then, ask you, fair reader, brought about the organ failure?! Well, the esophageal membrane, prior to its own cauterization, had allowed into the bloodstream just that morning those allergens contained in a single candied peanut that Dink had mistook for an 800 milligram tablet of ibuprofen, and only now was he being affected.)

And still the pavement undulated and flowed.

CHAPTER 2

The sniveling, sniffling seven-sphinctered sphinx

Plopped with aplomb amongst Platonic plumbers

Alas! romanced he not, but (quoth the lynx),

"Do not ye numb the sphincters' seven numbers!"

That frackering, freemongerous freak of freedom,

That bulbous, bilious, beakless lynx of old,

Spawned in the Massachusetts town of Needham,

With vile violence, cried, "My tale's all told!"

—Dandur Flandendrick,

The Profaning of the Færie Romance

BOOVVARIUN Palestriniac was emotionally invested in even the more sloppily produced of the countless gritty documentaries about new-wave accordionist Jovantrick Spatchel and his controversial wig-making cartel.

He sat slouched in the prosaic institutional chair he had looted from the nearby abandoned elementary school. Sitting in it, running his fingers along the textured molded plastic, made him nostalgic and brought back thoughts of cheery teachers with their overpowering perfume and the musty rubber smell of the gymnasium and the nearby mopwater-infused cafetorium. There was absolutely no need for him to revisit Episode 14 of the second season of *Polka Nouveau: Scissors Scandals*, as he had every word of dialogue and every jaunty intonation of the featured Hohner Gola 414 accordion written on his heart.

Storper Mullignoc, Boov's dumpily-built bumbling bungler of a housemate, called him out on this.

"Shut up!" cried the other defensively.

"That I can't!" snorted Storper. "You're wearing the commemorative wig right now. This has to stop, man. I can't sleep at night on account of your unending screams at the television."

"Just you wait. It's only a matter of time before you find your own spiritual squeezebox."

"Oh, I've got mine, Boovis. Ever heard of voiceover screenplays for high-budget nature films?" Storper went running off, returning moments later with a stack of wide-ruled notebook paper covered in coffee stains and scribblings written in purple crayon.

Palestriniac's eyes lit up, and his manner softened.

"Whoa! Let's hear some, Storps!"

"Really? Okay, well . . ." He shuffled his rumpled papers and began:

"'The hot heat of the wild wilderness—'"

"That's the stupidest thing I ever heard!"

"Shut up! You're the worst! Dink was right about your

pettiness when he was talking trash about you the other day—only it turns out it wasn't his talk but *you* who's the trash!"

Boov's wretched compadre ran off in tears, only to slip on a writing slate that had been looted much earlier from a much older abandoned school. He skinned his elbow on some old broken chalk when he fell, and his tears multiplied. When he hyperventilatively surveyed his injury, he wondered at the scrapes, which looked for all the world like a fragment of Cyrillic script. Boovvariun likewise marveled, but only for a moment, for now came the infamous bit where Jovantrick Spatchel irreverently played a Piazzolla tango in an uproariously Bohemian style on an English concertina. It was not to be missed.

Just then they heard a knock at the door. Mullignoc remained incapacitated on the ground, as his wound now resembled the bold lettering of some barbaric land. The peruke-posturing oom-pah dilettante *par excellence* therefore answered the door.

Blinx Doptik stood outside. Outside the door, that is, to the house of somebody else—and long ago, at that!

But it turned out that the knock heard by B.P. and S.M. was nothing more than the thwack of a well-aimed Sunday paper that now rested on the welcome mat, which, as it happened, was actually more of a phosphorescent astroturf trimming illicitly scissored out of the courtyard of a derelict night school building.

CHAPTER 3

He stubbered along like a stopian strynx,

Bliftered about in the wherves of the winx,

Till at midday, no later, no earlier, but then,

He summoned Vektruvialist, a kind hen.

—*Rigneus Duperson,* The Euphratean Gaucho

KLAUS wriggled unto liberty, and Vleffix, having been thoroughly had (and by a large, loving rodent too!), fidgeted with her electromechanical limb; she saw nothing better to do, and the guinea pig's brushing against it in his scurry to the floorboard, it was true, had knocked its retractable copper exhaust pipes awry.

"What happened to you anyway?" asked Dink clumsily. (His multiple organs, having failed for a time, rallied, and in the end, succeeded admirably.)

The Visigoth coolly replied, "The minute gravitational forces of the rings of Saturn have a way of elongating one's body via expansion at the joints—and of leaving the density and strength of one's bones greatly deteriorated. Here, look this way."

She unexpectedly grabbed and unbent his broken nose to fix it, just like in the movies. But it didn't work, and it didn't even make a crunchy noise. Really, the brokenness of his nose wasn't crooked enough to need unbending in the first place. Some half-coagulated blood goopily oozed out and that was it. This made Flapple's eyes water and he sneezed, wiping the whole mess on what used to be a monochromatic hot-pink sleeve. Vleffix turned away in disgust and dry-heaved a little bit. All this happened in about five seconds.

Dink picked the conversation right back up as if nothing had happened: "Really? That explains so much!"

Vleffix recovered. "It explains nothing."

"Huh?"

She sighed. "Or maybe the WNBA isn't for everybody, and a unicyclist once shattered my tibia in an attempt to ride under my legs."

"I did that?!"

"Of course not, you buffoon. But it's enough to have my vengeance on unicyclists in general."

"But you did go to Saturn, right?"

"Of course not."

"But then how are you so tall?"

"Stop talking."

Vleffix had had enough. She picked up her fake leg, drew it to her lips, and exhaled powerfully. A purple smoke plumed from the exhaust pipes, awry though they were, and Dink's sensory faculties not only failed him, but interpreted inversely those stimuli to which they were subjected: The cloudless sky he observed as orange, and the purple smoke promptly appeared yellow; and with rindy-bitterness did his olfactory awareness perceive the salty-sweetness of the PayDays and Baby Ruths that crammed the glove compartment; and with anxiety and melancholia did his ears receive that little song Bobby McFerrin wrote as it was sung note for note over the Philco AM/FM receiver. Dink was a mess, and therefore, in his own eyes, cleanliness incarnate.

"Where's the knob?" he whimpered, groping at the dashboard with his feet rather than his hands. At last, with a counterclockwise twist to the newfound knob using the inside heel of his right shoe (he wore Jellies), he reduced the volume to a whisper, which very nearly deafened him. But Vleffix proceeded to shut it off.

"There."

"Where?"

She closed her eyes and shook her wirehair-helmeted head, which made a sound like a dozen Slinkies descending stairs. She paused for a moment and then tried again.

"There: the radio's off. What's the matter? Don't you like Bob Marley?" She smirked.

"Oh, it's better now. I guess the effects of your purple haze wore off. And that wasn't even Bob Marley, Quirff—or Hendrix, for that matter."

"Bruce Springsteen. Whatever. I don't even like music."

"But Springsteen's not even *remotely*—Wait, what? Like, any music?"

"None."

"How can you not like music?" Dink wasn't many things, but one thing he indeed was, just then, was incredulous.

"It's nothing but organized sound. Just as a file cabinet is nothing but organized files. And I don't like file cabinets."

As Master Flapple was pondering whether one can truly dislike a file cabinet, unanswered questions flooded his compromised brain.

"Here's the thing, your majesty. You hit me with your car, you made me run like a Flintstone in your grunge-era sedan only to put it in park and liquefy the street for locomotion, you tried to poison me with a candy bar you ate half of, and then you lovingly feared for my life while getting frightened by my guinea pig as he wiggled around, all squirrely and wonderful. So what's behind it all? Huh?"

"I've been waiting for you to ask. And the rings of Saturn do come into play, obviously. But first you must understand that I am a delegate of the Rhapsodic Council of none other than Carpentrius, fibersmith-forger."

"Wood fiber?"

"Carbon fiber—and optical. Now listen. I had to take measures to ensure you would quickly develop a sufficiently sturdy disposition for handling the truth. The pavement only appears to be moving; reverting it to its molten state allows us to remain utterly stationary—absolutely stationary—while the earth continues to rotate just beneath us."

"Wait a minute. Do you mean to say that we only appear to be heading due west, and that Uzbekistan will arrive at this car in 12 hours' time?"

"I can't believe it. Yes, that's exactly what I mean."

Dink beamed a big, dumb smile. He cracked open the New

Coke and guzzled it down. He belched up some of the ensuing foam, having forgotten how warm sodas behave, and it fizzed forth from his nostrils. Quirff, who might be a heroine after all, continued:

"But on account of the dream state you entered when you inhaled my purpling anti-haze, time did fly, and we have sat motionlessly for well over 11-and-a-half hours already, so our wait is nearly over. The ruins of Kantubek on the former island Vozrozhdeniya lie amidst the sifting sands of the dried Aral Sea, and behold! even now they race toward us."

This would be right up Boover's alley, thought Flapple. He crushed the empty New Coke can on his forehead.

CHAPTER 4

The blithering, thrombular dimbulus quat,

O you anti-tiquated mid-thumb,

Of Rimbeus (quantrescent shimberous gnaut)

Soon precludes the quart-heifer quite numb.

Now, if shirkings force-flink the flan-flatchering flamb

O' the clamberist, piftiest florist,

The inferiorest lepidopterist wrist

Was un-Christmasèd harkly before us!

—Franticloz Bodego, Culled Suet

D OOP *Voobiddy had been married to Corpostula Speemyin-dricks for over eighty years when he left her for a freshly-centenarian floozy called Blarkturia Chambextico. It was seemingly none other than mercenary Farpster Wheese who proceeded to steal Doop's yacht, Yon Kipper, from an East River marina near Battery Park and sail it full throttle at 40 knots or more, colliding with the headlands of a shore not at all far from Ellis Island; but the after-*

math of the explosion, alas, revealed the twinkly skeleton of Dame Speemyindricks at the helm.

Just beyond where her sparkly skull lay danced a pair of buckled shoes bedecked in spatterdashes, powered by merrily jigging legs affixed to the torso that supported the head whose wryly wily smiling face was, clearly, that of Jovantrick Spatchel. His arms were there too, and they and their hands played the accordion. His henchman Sweat Barves ran about him in tight circles, feverishly snapping shots with his Polaroid camera. Conspicuously, Voobiddy sat upon a high tree stump in the middle distance, kicking his lanky legs and fidgeting with his handlebar mustache.

Boovvariun Palestriniac buzzed his lips flatulently with glee at the familiar sight of Spatchel—who had done it again! But suddenly he witnessed the piercing blink of the TV set's cathode rays terminating, with the accompanying zapping sound.

"Hey! What gives?"

"I give—give a hoot, that is! . . . *Not!*" Storper Mullignoc glowed with self-satisfaction.

Palestriniac tossed his head to throw back the hair of the wig he still wore, communicating a gesture of girlish defiance. Though his eyes did grow misty.

"Whatever. I just saw that one two days ago anyway. So there!"

"There shmair! Hey, isn't 'hoot' a great word?"

"I don't think it's great. At all."

"All shmaul!"

"Know what? You smell terrible today."

And so they expostulated with one another. Somewhere in their back yard crowed a cock, stolen recently from a school of farming. The wind grew cold.

* * *

It might very well be of no small interest to the reader that among Storper's rumpled papers was poetry, among it this plagiarized nugget from the Edwardian-era "Bard of Barbados," Josephorius Josepharianator:

LXIV: SPRING RESERVOIR SLIME.

Vleemee Gawbstt the tortoise

Was a man of high ideals

But when his shell turned inside-out

He used his spleens for wheels

Such means of locomotion

Also brought about ingestion

But how he would get rightside-out remained the real question.

"Reverting to my former state,"

Pontificated he,

"Would disallow my newfound

Sensory-immunity.

But still, I think it brilliant

T'have my face outside my brain;

This feeling of inversion

Causes no uncertain pain."

And thus he slinked into a hole
That narrowed at its nadir,
Effecting bodily prolapse
As it cinched and pinched his rear.
But happy restoration
Only prologued further strife
As he was sucked into the sky.
He was sure to miss his wife.

* * *

You might recall, reader, that the wind had grown cold just outside Palestriniac and Mullignoc's run-down, half-occupied duplex in the ungated community of Whistlesome Warblery Thistlewoods.

"Close the window, Storpid."

Disarmingly, he obeyed. The downward-sliding lower sash, however, got bound up just an inch shy of the sill and in its obstinacy there remained, while the upper sash spontaneously loosed itself of the head jamb and began sliding on account of a developing warp in a muntin that had progressed to a bowing of the abutting rail. It didn't help that the side jambs, with their (startlingly) debris-free channel casements, allowed for perhaps a little too much clearance for the stile in its entirety, though the exterior sill, and the stool and apron, remained in perfect condition. No sooner had this happened than a wall of tar-soaked gravel slammed into every east-facing window, obliterating the glazes themselves, reducing the windows to mere cavities in the rapidly deteriorating walls, which very shortly thereafter succumbed to the precipitous asphalt cataract that fell not downward but westward.

Beyond all reason, the clownish housemates had climbed atop their dining room table to wrestle one another the moment young Storper's God-given scent was insulted, and it was from the tabletop that he had reached to close the window in the first place. And so they avoided the impact of the torrent, getting caught up *on* it instead. I say "*on* it" advisedly, as they only ever skimmed and tumbled about the topmost surface of what they observed to be a sort of blurred, narrow, grey-black band of rubble extending infinitely before and behind them in a perfectly straight line with indistinct edges to their left and right that suggested a terrifyingly finite width of mere meters.

Mullignoc fell off and died.

CHAPTER 5

I've empathy for entropy;
Its essence is corruption
How I identify with thee,
O nonchalant eruption
Of fatalistic fantasies,
Reductionistic liberties
And all eventualities
Defying interruption

—Silhendric Frantrix, Ha'penny-Cute Mutiny

TAKE off your sunglasses already. You're ridiculous."

Dink did so, revealing large, vacuous eyes of a boring color. He looked out the window, attempting in vain to observe his surroundings. That upon which the car was situated was, in fact, unmade pavement in an ultra-low orbit exactly counter to the earth's own rotation. Quirff called it motionlessness, and her utterly unremarkable companion regarded it as such accordingly; but wondrous Klaus betrayed the physical reality, whatever it was, with his complete loss of bowel control.

She picked up the warm, cozy mammal in disgust and threw him out the window. Immediately Dink's hands were on Vleffix's neck in a choke hold. He recoiled when her riveted tin neckpiece became scalding hot.

"Relax, Flapple. Our destination has arrived. Your foul guinea pig is relieving himself even now in the sand."

"Oh! Good. Hey, wouldn't you say that *we* are the destination, though? Since we're stationary?"

"Ugh. I guess."

They exited the vehicle and traversed the sands to the ghost town. Too, Boovvariun Palestriniac disembarked from the otherworldly levitating treadmill, which, all things considered, had commenced its solidification and realignment with our planet's spin quite gently. He careened onto his brother from another mother Dink Flapple, sending him to a face plant at some 400 miles per hour. They were both just fine, though.

"Hey Dinkus! Whatcha listening to?" He pulled at an earpiece of the headphones that hung about his neck, still blasting his playlist of the complete cycle of Wagner's bloated operas transcribed for accordion orchestra. Boov was still in a state of complete shock and was unconsciously coping through idle chatter.

"Holy moly, roly-poly! A Spatchel special, no doubt!"

"Another frantic schtick of Jovantrick!" They high-fived.

The satisfyingly reverberant smack of their self-congratulatory little game of patty-cake echoed among the dilapidated Soviet structures, making one fall over in an implosion rife with toxic vapor. Quirff unhesitatingly spread her jumbo cape, stitched of steel wool, to shelter all three of them from the ensuing biological weaponry. She warned them to be still.

"And don't pick up any of those bulbous Campbell's Soup cans amidst the ruins," she added, "unless you want botulism."

But Dink had already somehow opened a tomato soup can and chugged it. Palestriniac's wig was now making him quite sweaty, and the traumatic events of the recent hours in combination with Flapple's spoiled soup stench proved too much for him. He fell into a faint, dreaming of the letter G in terrifyingly pure abstraction; of clouds that were actually numbers all along; and also, finally, of colors being verbs, and most intuitively too, in the casually irrefutable manner peculiar to dreams. "Undo unto. Fund frowned unfounded fun. Blob the bubble daub the dawdle," blued one cumulus which was none other than the number seventy-six.

Boov awoke drenched in perspiration. They were still beneath the woolen steel cape, which now glowed orange like an elaborate network of toaster coils.

"How long have I been asleep?"

Dink, with his sagging mouth circumscribed in red goop, replied, "Oh, I don't know. I didn't notice you were asleep."

"You fainted about nineteen seconds ago," said the tall, witchy woman. "And we should be good now." She drew back her cape, and it retracted into her hitherto unused jet pack, igniting it, presumably, via heated coil. And they were off.

Yes, they were all drawn aloft by Quirff's enigmatic power, and far below them they beheld a terrific gushing coruscation of water bursting forth from every door, window, and seam of the the forsaken 1993 Ford Taurus, immediately refilling and restoring the Aral Sea to its 1960s glory. Beheld also was Storper Mullignoc, immersed in the brand-new wetness, dog-paddling expeditiously.

Palestriniac's mounting stupefaction left him over-whelmed. He shook his head, mouth agape, as he rolled his eyes psychotically like a slapstick vintage cartoon predator. Finally he stated that which he knew to be true: "You died!—Come on, you're dead, Storper!"

"And what, so you're just gonna leave me behind?!"

They all stared blankly.

"Huh?!" persisted the deceased.

It wasn't without awkwardness that they all accepted his company. But that they did, and the blithe bunch, who kept abreast of one another in flight, were brought abreast also of the business of Vleffix and Dink, that being the quest to Carpentrius, fibersmith-forger.

* * *

Dink Bucephalus Flapple II—"It's not 'Junior,'" as he him-self says to all who would demur—was born on a railroad track and raised by a semi-retired beatboxer known only as dèçiB€L, who had little Dinky-doo on the streets selling pre-inflated tires to pram wholesalers and pre-inflated balloons to carnival barkers and part-time pro bono clowns. By the age of 12, he was the premier vendor of all things rubber and circular from Iowa to Wyoming, and by the age of 14 he had made his first million, which he summarily blew on king-sized candy bars and an eBay rock from Mount Sinai that purportedly had Moses' autograph on it. At 17, he happened upon his father, Dink Senior, at the local batting cages. Senior was wearing a tweed leisure suit with a sombrero and bunting every ball, so *II*, disgusted, and arrayed in a tux and tricorne himself, opted to treat him as a stranger, turning to him only to say, "Nice hat, *y ¡buen trabajo!*" before batting his last and driving to the next state instead of home.

His first and only unicycle was entirely bespoke, and he rose to the upper echelon of uni sportsmanship by the age of 20, even toying with experimental velocipede slacklining and penny farthing mountaineering. Dink had bovine (or perhaps equine) eyes of nondescript color and was for all intents and purposes chinless. He had medium-cropped, straight-as-straw hair of a greyish-blondish-brownish color—a sort of dishwater but less distinct—and a bouncy gait that accentuated his lanky near-six-foot build. His teeth were white and perfect, his voice like butter, and his broad grin primitive and dubious. There was an inexplicable air of naïve jadedness about him.

* * *

Anyway, our troop landed softly and of one accord on a tiny shoal in the midmost regions of the Indian Ocean. It was here that the asinine accordion aficionado finally had a chance to think. Boovvariun had seen with his own eyes how Storper fell to his death, how his torso exploded and his face went flying. *What evidence do I have of reality*, he thought, *beyond that of my own senses?* This line of thinking reminded him of Jacob Marley's visit to Ebenezer Scrooge, which reminded him of Jovantrick Spatchel's visit to Expesiastica Drourke. He smiled to himself gently and ran his fingers through the real human hair of his wig before checking himself and reexamining the predicament of Storper's existence. It was too late for further thought, though: Abruptly, Quirff performed an aggressive jumping-jack sort of move, wherewith three shovels ejected from her three extremities. Her bionic limb served as her own shovel, but she had no intention of using it.

"Start digging," said Quirff in a rather Vleffix tone of voice.

CHAPTER 6

Flibbertigibbety will-o'-the-wisp

Pickles and apples and air oh so crisp

Sanguine or phlegmatic, not psychosomatic

But dental appliance-borne lisp

Categorical imperatives most irreducible

Açaí, West Coast style, mixed up in a nice, juicy bowl

Inchoate first learnings and nascent, fresh earnings

As ruthlessly crisp as a crucible

—Spryttle Spheeniewryler,
   The Inevitabilitator's Futility

H EY Quirffy, what was even the point of stopping in those cool, creepy Soviet ruins on that former island of the former lower lobe of the Aral Sea?" said Dink, increasingly the voice of reason. He grabbed a shovel and pretended to work.

"Never call me that again," she hissed.

Quirff-without-a-'y' then paused for effect before continuing.

"I had reason to believe Carpentrius was there. Further, Mullignoc's death brought about the languishing sea's replenishment by way of my car, and besides, he needed a chance to catch up with us; I knew he would be close behind after our rendezvous with Palestriniac."

"How could you possibly have known that?"

"Just think of me as your guardian angel," said our beloved giantess, giving him a wink that jostled her wooden dentures nobody knew she had up until that point. They made an unsettling clicking sound. Klaus shivered.

Just beyond, or below, rather, on the long-forgotten Sunken Isle of Badrad Baldi, Carpentrius paced in a mannered, measured manner about his carpeted throne room. He was a Dickensian character, jovial, barrel chested, bedecked in a tawny nylon-lined robe of wild dog hide, and standing at least six feet tall, although his aquiline nose with flaring nostrils conferred upon him an added air of authority that seemed to make him even taller. His well-arranged alabaster teeth, often communicating a grin so uproariously good-natured it could have been Teddy Roosevelt's own, clenched a corncob pipe (packed only with the finest Virginia tobacco) which jutted nonchalantly out of a broad mouth sheltered beneath a luxuriant auburn mustache that terminated just shy of his ears. His abundant beard, replete with joyous curls, was made up of many thousands of ebullient hairs that disembarked from their follicles to venture a full seven inches beyond the epidermal borders of his strong chin. His fulvous eyes were the color of a tiger somehow shorn of its stripes. Carpentrius, fibersmith-forger, was orating:

"Abstemious reconnoitering has its forbearers. Justice, once again, indentures loquacity unto asymptotic curves." He looked about the room valiantly, but not without self-satisfaction. "Croissants do not the man make. Unmade, henceforth, are all indomitables. Flints and sticks upon the ceiling, aye, and even now tasks the capybara"—and he shot a quick, coy glance back and forth about his court—"but rather toothlessly!" He beamed a beautiful smile that was not toothless at all.

Hodezemiah Dweetle, courtier, entered from the antechamber. Carpentrius looked up with an air of alarmed derision and spake thus:

"Slob!"

"Wait, what—"

"Indeed it was, my little buffoon! Alas! and sassafras. Truly, yes."

"—I, uh, cannot say I fully understand thy line of reasoning, Your Grace, but submit I shall."

This last utterance went unheard, as Carpentrius was now rolling his tongue while letting loose a mellifluous bellow. The bestial sound erupting forth had an overwhelming robustness about it, much like Boris Karloff or Paul Robeson. Nothing like Fred Rogers, but a little bit like James Earl Jones and a lot like Topol, star of *Fiddler on the Roof.*

Abruptly he stopped, and after scat-singing his favorite sea chantey[1]—he had only been warming up for this, just previously, with that hefty tongue trill—he muttered,

"Horticulturalistics abide. Scrape utterly, and tenon-bomb the Tannenbaum tanners. Now go, and ye shan't—won't!—de-pants the boat."

The butler came from out of nowhere. "Say, that reminds me: How shall one spell my newly-coined word starting with a 'w' but rhyming with 'pant'?"

Dweetle offered, "'Want?'"

"Well, seemingly so, but you have just said what must be spelled just like 'want,' and it must rhyme with 'can't,' you see."

"'W'ant'?" phonated the fibersmith-forger himself.

"Ah! Why, yes—precisely! The way you have said it is spelled most aptly, Your Excellency!" The butler was rather overcome with gladness at this point, and he kissed the ringed right hand of his master before backing away, curtsying, and backing up some more until he fell down some stairs.

Then receptionist Blastula Harbigganotham announced in her characteristically gruff manner the approach of four un-invited guests from above. Dweetle gasped, and his double-chin bulged as he dropped his jaw. He attempted a running jump out of the room and fell short; the antechamber re-mained a good five yards away.

Fifty-six feet directly above Carpentrius's footstool the soggy shoal sand started sinking suddenly, and Vleffix shouted, "Now!" Everyone did nothing all at once. But then Storper, punchy from the lack of sleep since death, thought, *Why not?* and dove straight into the new sinkhole, multiply-ing its size and power to such a degree that they were all sucked down.

The fibersmith-forger's elevated bare feet became dusty, then sandy, then buried in people. He tilted his head slightly and raised an eyebrow, looking straight to the person who spoke to him first. It was his servant Quirff.

"Welcome to us," she said with gravitas.

"Why not!" replied Carpentrius without hesitation. "Hot wine!" He looked about delightedly.

Palestriniac and Flapple exchanged doubtful glances, but the woman with the cybertronic leg glared so fiercely that they said nothing.

Mullignoc, however, wasn't looking at her. "Hey, why aren't you sick from that tomato soup, Dink?"

The timing of this remark was so bad that the one being addressed was caught off guard and forgot to continue holding his tongue: "What? *Who cares?* What even made you think of that?"

The sudden movements accompanying Dink's sudden blurt spooked guinea pig Klaus. He jumped out of his master's fanny pack and scurried across the room at eight miles per hour, running onto Hodezemiah Dweetle's prostrate body and lying down upon his buttocks. The collapsed courtier made a brief effort to lift his head off of the floor and turn to see, but quickly gave up and lowered his face once again. But not before Vleffix made eye contact with him.

"Dweetle, is that you? I can't believe this."

He made only a muffled murmur into the luxurious carpeting.

"You summon me on behalf of the Council only to provide misinformation about a Kantubek rendezvous. And yet you don't seem surprised to see us here. What else? Do we even need dear Dink Flapple?"

He lifted his head this time: "I could not have anticipated the turn of events that led us all here, but it is true, yes, that I knew it could only have been you and your posse who suddenly showed up just now. And Flapple, you and I both know, is the key to unlocking the riddle of Saturn's rings."

But just then, Jeptunianizer the Man burst forth from the ground in a veritable eruption! He wore only bluejeans. "Rhapsodic Council, unite!" he hollered, and charged at Carpentrius, who was now translucent and immaterial. The two men, instead of colliding, merged into a newly corporeal superman who, though he bore the very appearance of our kingly forger of fiber, unmistakably possessed a new quality that defied articulation. The same sonorous voice spoke, but now with the light of human reason.

"I feel like a man again!"

CHAPTER 7

Those dubblesome nubblers have dweebled their last,

Betwixt cornucopias fulsome and vast!

If hadn't they, surely, I daren't admire

The vorvixxes, doubtless, they fruppiously conspire!

Whence vubbiously vortured the Sprechstimmer sprockets

Amidst the fine lint in mine own doozy pockets?!

Anon and allez and ahoy did they spreech,

Don splatzum and figgerdeeroo—out of reach.

—Sir Kitbraicurres, Hypercubus Chasmos

I T'S good to have you back, O Carpentrius," said Dweetle warmly, just after getting up when he realized he was uninjured.

"Thanks," he said, distractedly. He was examining his fingertips in search of hangnails. He could have sworn he had one.

Dink ventured to speak. "Uh, first . . . do I have to be polite because you're the King of America or something?"

He looked up abruptly, having abandoned his search. "Not

even close!" he replied fun-lovingly. He tickled Dink playfully under his left armpit, and Dink had to stomp his left foot to suppress a laugh.

"Alright, cool. So what in the name of all things decent was that that we just saw?"

"Ah. Well, my forge is well below the earth's crust, and it occupies my Jeptunianizer-self constantly. But I need a presence here too, and that's where the shell-man comes in. All he can do, really, is make free associations with words, and even then, he grasps only the sounds of them. The gift of language he possesses not, and his interactions with his fellow man are purely bestial, I can assure you."

With that last statement, he held up his hand demonstratively, but Storper completely misunderstood and gave him a high-five, which Carpentrius gladly accepted—and with a spirited hoot of affirmation too, bless him!

He then clapped his own hands and rubbed them together enthusiastically. "Who's hungry?"

They all headed to the den, and before they knew it, the friendly forger, donning a brilliant white chef's hat and spatulae multifarious, was cooking up a vat of chili and grilling weenies. Fresh buns emerged from an oven no one even knew was there. No man of any age has ever laid such food upon his taste buds as our crew did theirs. Chili dogs galore. Yes, steaming, juicy chili dogs on sloppy-joe-soggy buns. Moderation was perhaps the only thing off the table—which was lined with a cloth of the crispest linen, and chock-full of the most disarmingly lovely piles of chili dogs any mortal or angel has ever experienced: piles of abundance, falling and flopping all over each other. Two, three, seven—it mattered not; any and every chili dog was a chili dog any and every guest had any and every right to. To partake was to rejoice in life itself; to exult in one's very being, and in seasons most varied, too: to savor the chilly days and dog days alike.

Boovvariun wept with rapt tenderness as chili ran down the sides of his mouth, a half-finished chili dog in each hand. Storper, dead, contented himself standing atop the table barefoot, pulverizing the dogs under the weight of his feet as smushed wads seeped up between his toes, and letting the cheese of the chili brush across the tops of those same feet, leaving them nice and shiny. Dink, on the ground, wallowed in a forty-dog mass, gently turning his head to eat of it at his leisure. His hair and clothes were caked in congealed, meaty goo, and he thought of his carnival days. Quirff completely immersed her head in the vat of chili and aspirated its contents, letting her lungs fill with the spiced brown sludge as a far-superior substitute for air. Blue-tinged circuitry in her electrobionic leg glowed brightly. Her dunk splashed warm grease all over Hodezemiah's cheeks and glasses and he stepped backward in a start, tripping over Dink and falling headlong toward the linoleum tilework below, but his face, now slick, slipped on the floor and glided into the air, and he fell back onto his feet. As for Carpentrius, he was overjoyed just to look on, and an expression of sheer exuberance came over his countenance.

Then they all got cleaned up, but remained in an inebriate stupor on account of the transcendent chili dogs. The fiber-smith-forger knew just what to do. He pulled at the starter cord on his gasoline-powered mechanical guitar, revving it up on G minor until it roared.

"Whew-whee!!"

He was his own smoke machine as he down-shifted unexpectedly to a sumptuous G-flat major seventh chord only to hit the accelerator, leaving everyone in awe. But the throttle locked up, frustratingly, and before he could hit the shutoff valve, he broke a string, tripping the main breaker. It was at this point his instrument started overflowing, and his repeated flushing only made it worse. Sparks were flying.

"Anyone got some Drano?" queried the freshly-drenched forger sheepishly. Before Mullignoc could proudly present his own perfectly-preserved free sample, still stashed in the fifth pocket of his jean shorts, Carpentrius continued: "Well, is everyone awake and alert, anyway? We have much to discuss, Council."

CHAPTER 8

Amidst the blessèd cit'zens lived a dork
Who ate his victuals wholly with a spork
"The tineless spoon," he muttered, like a fool,
"Proves less than satisfactory a tool."
And yet, he, worthless moron that he was,
Denied the fork its place in spite of us:
"I'd rath'r a cradle to embrace my food;
The fork's sleek tines betray an attitude
Of spartan functionality so rude
Beyond sensorium, not unlike the quark."
That lepton-brain sups therefore with the spork.

—*Arjeptra Calexdonicon,* Collected Cutlery Invective

H E grabbed an old towel that was lying around to wrap about his waist and did a *California switch* right there in front of them into some bike shorts and a Nantucket-red polo shirt. He jiggled his limbs to regroup.

"Ah. Better. Now, first of all—"

But the butler reappeared, again as if out of nowhere.

"Excellency, have you any suggestion for me, in my correspondence with the technologist, for a word that serves as an apt descriptor for the smell of sound?"

Carpentrius winced in psychic pain. "Uh . . . 'rainbowish.'"

The underling's mouth popped open in a silent scream.

But the forger remained unfazed. "That it is, or nothing."

"*But sir!*"

"What I have said is nothing other than that which must be," he snapped. "Now off with you, m'lad."

The butler, shaking his head in disbelief and awe, once again backed away as he exited the room, ever facing his royal superior out of deference, until he could walk backward no more and, in complete bewilderment, entered a heretofore-unnoticed turnstile. The whole company watched him for the better part of a minute until he found his way out with a backward somersault.

The fibersmith-forger shimmied his face in the manner a wet mongrel shakes off. "Gol-*ly*, where was I? Ah yes. First of all: welcome, initiates. You are sufficiently fed for the ten-day fast now required of us as we sojourn on Daphnis, ring shepherd of Saturn. Dink B. Flapple, as leader of the pack, you shall decide just when we depart—though the *how* shall be left to me, as the departure precedes the arrival only with great skill and experience."

"Whuh?" returned Dweetle, still in a state of confusion from falling off of his face. "Do you mean to say, sire, that we risk arriving before we leave if we are too hasty?"

"And how," added Quirff, "can that be, Carpentrius? My powers are great and many, it cannot be denied, but do you mean to tell us you have accomplished travel at a super-relativistic velocity?"

The 'smith-forger placed his hands on his hips, thumbs-forward as if stretching his back, and threw his head back to heave a great sigh. "You think this has to do with science, you dweeb?"

"Let's just go right now," Dink said with a withering smirk.

"Just as well." Carpentrius paused and met everyone's eyes in turn: "Perpend."

Then, with the startling finesse of an illusionist, he grabbed two chalkboard erasers from Palestriniac's inner coat pockets—Boov had stolen them from a Montessori school that had closed just the year before—and began to beat them together briskly, filling the space with a billowing cloud of dust. With his right foot he scooted a large oval wall mirror out from underneath the dining table as he continued to clap the erasers. Flapple and Mullignoc looked at each other (faux-)knowingly and now felt pumped up, so they quickly high-fived and just as quickly fell back so as not to miss any-thing. From the hole in the collapsed ceiling a shaft of sun-light broke through, for the angle of the sun had become just so, and landed on the mirror. The dust cloud, of course, ren-dered the light beam visible and seemingly tangible all along its length, so when the forger stomped through the mirror and the reflection of the beam remained, extending beyond the broken shards and descending, as it were, through the floor, it almost did not come as a surprise.

Carpentrius, stooped on the ground amid the shattered glass, took hold of the line of light and slid down.

"My erasers!" shrieked Boovvariun.

CHAPTER 9

Gossamer saucers! For tea or for flying!
Stout dental flossers, now dead-set on dying,
Lest, livid with living, and over-forgiving,
And anti-symmetrically riven with fibbing,
Their gibbering gibes and tongue-in-cheek ribbing
Get well out of hand and provoke unto crying
Those saucers whose gossamer disallows flying;
Good only for teatime, then washing, then drying.

—Credensic Brimp, Flightlessness Underground

T HE others joined our phantasmagoric forger after they had a good scream—Storper Mullignoc's, though, could hardly be categorized a scream, as his voice, even before he passed away, was just about as deep as Barry White's, so he let loose a sound like the horn of a freight train—and Dink, at his turn, having passed out of the sensibly terrestrial and into the intuitively preternatural, dimly observed an incomprehensible, seemingly unrelated series of visual stimuli.

Straight ahead was a brilliant, hazy vertical band, fading at both sides, albeit asymmetrically, to complete blackness. Flapple looked up as well as down and only saw the same, but directly in front of him in the middle distance, the haze seamlessly sharpened to a suspension of phosphorescent gravel, apparently motionless. He too seemed stationary, at least as far as vertical movement was concerned, but suddenly he rotated about his pole of dusty light—was it sediment?—and, now facing the other way, a soft, milky luminescence dominated the entirety of his field of vision. No sooner had he taken notice of this than he began somehow to tumble, and the vertical band came into sight once again, shifting, now nearly horizontal. Then darkness of such totality it was almost palpable. And then nothing but the milkiness again! All along, Dink experienced utter silence. And an overpowering smell distinctly like the sharp breath of a newborn hound.

His ridiculous end-over-end motion quieted to a drifting lateral rotation, and he then laid eyes on an immense oblong boulder amid the gravel-haze, which was now no longer a foreshortened band or ribbon but an expansive plane of variegated parallel lines, oceanic in its proportions. The rocky mass was in fact within a sort of gap, a thick stripe of darkness occurring within the brilliant stripes of granular haze. And he sensed his own motion, and it was that of sinking underwater: slowly, inevitably—toward the boulder, which was turning out to be far, far more than a boulder. The moon Daphnis shepherded the rings of Saturn, and it was upon this Saturnian satellite that Dink and the others softly, ever so softly, alighted.

* * *

Quirff fired the boosters integrated into the undersides of her platform shoes (instantly vaporizing the goldfish that had swum about in the heel of the left one), allegedly to facilitate a soft landing, but this was needless and she knew it; she just wanted to look cool in front of Carpentrius. But she paid for her vanity: The boosters did far more than offset the microgravity of the tiny moon, and she had all the appearance of a pair of underwear being hurled into a wind tunnel.

With a small grin and a distant look in his eyes, the executive forger of all known fibersmithies, that highest-ranking smith of all fiberforges, popped his collar just then, producing from beneath it a horseshoe-shaped boomerang composed of braided strands of carbon fiber and nylon monofilament. Further, it was chrome-plated, befitting of an impromptu pseudo-cyborg rescue mission. Unexpectedly, he wadded it up with both hands and then released it. So forcefully did it uncrinkle itself that it was propelled into the dark vacuum above. A few short moments later, Vleffix fell, the boomerang-collar wrapped about the front of her neck. The chrome finish of Carpentrius's doohickey was now rainbow-tinged, as if stained by fire or fuel, and our lady's cheeks were flushed in precisely the same way.

Boovvariun Palestriniac recovered his purloined erasers, which the forge-smith of fiber had had to drop in order to pop his collar. (He had been hugging the chalkdust-sunlight-Saturnring pole in fireman fashion, without the use of his hands, which had clutched those erasers all along—out of absolute necessity, apparently.) Safely stowed now, the erasers' splendid adventure came to an inglorious and inauspicious end. The still-wigged man wiped his dusty hands on the ground, which was not only far dustier, but made only of dust. Boov sneezed. His wig fell off altogether, face down on the ground, but received a much-needed powdering in the process. He replaced it nimbly, but sneezed again.

"Bless you," said Quirff, embarrassed once again unto politeness.

"Bless you, uh . . ." said Storp, faltering with the realization of the awkwardness of being second-blesser, "—uh, for that second sneeze." He had only made it more awkward, and, in desperation to save face, cried, "And bless all of you—so I never even have to say it anymore again! Or none of us do. Does! None of us . . ." He buried his hands in his face.

Boov put his arm around him, but recoiled in disgust. For Storper Mullignoc was dead. So he patted his back instead, though just once.

Mullignoc glowered. "Guys, just pretend I'm still alive, will you? I'm basically the same as before."

Dink looked at him, squinting wisely and with eyebrows raised enthusiastically. "You're, like, *exactly* the same."

"There you go! So everybody, just act natural."

They sure tried, but it was all they could do to keep their blood from boiling on account of the lack of atmospheric pressure, and they kept being pummeled by the particulate matter of Saturn's rings into which the moon on which they stood was intermittently plowing.

"All done with our sojourn! Ten Daphnis-days have come and gone already!" bellowed Carpentius.

"What a dumb planet," muttered Dink Flapple inaccurately.

* * *

Years ago, Dink had smuggled a unicycle onto the moon (Earth's) and was riding it around as a publicity stunt, but it backfired horribly in the Marius Hills region on the near side as Dink went careening into a pit and tore a hole in the crotch of a $225,000 space suit that had been borrowed for the occasion from stuntstronaut Slamme Gardombo.

It was Boovvariun Palestriniac who bailed him out of debtors' prison and sweet-talked Gardombo into welcoming Flapple back into the Historic Velocipede Aeronautics Confederation just in time for its Sesquicentennial Convention, throwing in his own dandy-horse uniform with accordion-spangled epaulets to seal the deal. Palestriniac was merely an acquaintance of Flapple's at the time, but the former had taken a shining to Dink a whole twelve months before when he had first beheld the man in his bespoke bellows-driven monocycle, a vehicle ridden inside its one tremendous wheel and propelled by compressing and expanding a giant squeeze-box with the knees. (Our intrepid cyclist had already sold his patent to "The Grand Slamme," who was kind enough to allow Dink to showcase the prototype there at the 149th Annual HVAC Convention in Qaanaaq, Greenland that very first year before it hit the global market to obscenely spectacular acclaim.)

They had then (at the 150th) run into each other at the food trucks, and, having made quick re-introductions, laughed themselves sick with recollections of the chicanerous antics of the immortal Jovantrick Spatchel. They went on to talk wigs for a while before asking each other if the other would be the other's best friend, and were delighted when the other accepted the other's offer. Dink even wore Boov's wig for the remainder of the day, and Boov, Dink's beanie.

With a clever joint business venture off the ground a mere six months later, one could never have foreseen the degree of innovation that ensued: rubberized waistcoats for all-weather downhill log-rolling with improved traction; cravats with built-in tire pumps for the gentleman on the go; wind-wigs built to be removed and whirled as a means of propulsion for the lazy roller skater; and, of course, motorized pants. Yes, their flops proved financially catastrophic, but they parted ways amicably, each a little wiser than they had been before, and they remain the best of friends to this very day.

* * *

"But wait!" cried Dink. "Where the *heck* is Klaus?"

All eyes turned to the heretofore forgotten Hodezemiah Dweetle, whose whimpers had suddenly become audible amid the stunned silence. His eyes and double-chin bulged wildly, as he stood frozen in slack-jawed horror.

Klaus, having heard his beautiful name, had jumped out of the commodious back pocket of Dweetle's JNCO jeans, but *into*, rather than out of, his pants, and came tearing out of the pathetic man's right pant leg, no worse for the wear, but in fact better: he now sported Dweetle's beaded ankle bracelet as a winsome collar.

"What a guy!" addressed the now teary eyed Flapple to his remarkable pet, and he stooped down and gathered him in his arms, giving him a squeeze. Klaus groaned with pleasure. Then, in a flash, he stowed the guinea pig back in his beanie.

"Ahem."

"Yes, O Carpentrius?" breathed Palestriniac, with hands clasped as in prayer.

But it was Quirff who was standing on the regal throat-clearer's foot, and when she realized this, she overcorrected by detaching her entire leg—yes, it was that one—hopping backward, and replacing it. A nervous laugh escaped her like the scraping of metal against plastic within a cheap appliance.

"So let's go, why don't we?" she shrilled.

"Well, *now* we *can*," grunted the forger, deeply offended.

CHAPTER 10

"And what's all this dwonkling I hear?" said old Sprank.

"It's fritzing and sprinking my postular flank!"

Of the none who did answer, still less winkled true—

And how that old dinkling derrière flew!

Devise all the childers, now; varp the fine vooties!

Antiggle the bleemer of all divine blooties.

Alas! and did not every jartle gambivver?

Go, therefore, to Sprank—before shymies ye shiver!

—Aplomb Mopdickerssen, The Closest Shave (1920)

CARPENTRIUS, fibersmith-forger, dropping to his knees and bracing his fists on the ground, began headbutting the surface of the Saturnian satellite until it suddenly gave way in the manner of a trap door with hinges situated to the rear. Indeed, he swung down and forward exactly ninety degrees but fell no further; the tips of his toes were now flush with Daphnis's surface and the rest of him was underground, only just. He now stood, not up, but sideways upon the wall of his hole, which somehow left his entire upper body obscured. Only his heels and calves were visible, as he stood facing the direction of the moon's core. His flesh had taken on an oddly uniform red hue, as if one was viewing him through red cellophane. He began to walk (from the mutual perspective of Dink, Quirff, Boovvariun, Storper, and Hodezemiah Dweetle) in a purely downward direction.

Seeing the fun results of headbutting the ground, and knowing they really had to be going anyway, Boov and Storp followed the forger's lead, and it wasn't long before Dink succumbed as well. He enjoyed the pleasing crunch of the bit of ground beneath him giving way. *This must be what a graham cracker feels like when it's broken in half,* he thought sagely. Vleffix and Dweetle looked at each other with expressions of sardonic resignation and then followed the others.

If these last two were jaded Rhapsodic Councilors on just another interdimensional mission, Dink was his plain old self, and *man* was he *pumped.*

"This is like Uncle Bonck's wine cellar, only with its own laws of gravity! And everything's red now . . . like we're looking through 3-D glasses with one eye closed!—*Wait:* Am I seeing in 3-D now?!"[2]

Quirff retched in a fit of supercilious disgust. "Ugh. Hey Dink, here's an idea: Look behind you and tell me what you see."

He looked back, raising one eyebrow and grinning a crooked half-smile, knowing full well that he would be looking up out the trap door thingy into the heavens. But when he looked back, and forward again, and all about, he realized that they were situated upon an interminable featureless plane whose surface shone a very dim ruby-red that, rather than offering a horizon of any kind, faded into a bleak emptiness on all sides. Above (that is, opposite the direction of the new gravity) was neither roof nor sky but indistinct darkness. And yet, peculiarly, it felt cramped. It felt to Flapple like an empty nightclub without walls.

Vleffix laughed caustically, for she knew she was a whole lot smarter than old Dink. Dink shot a defensive glance back at her.

"No going back now. Welcome to Hell," she sneered.

"Vleffix, leave him alone," muttered Carpentrius. He turned to look at Señor Flapple. "We're not in Hell, fine Dink. We're just traversing Meridian Apollonis, one of many monochromatic y-axis worlds. Ah!"

Stopping abruptly, he plopped down on the ground to perform the same head-banging maneuver as before, but this time he took care to reorient himself ninety degrees clockwise from the inward direction in which they had all been walking. The down-swinging trap door motion thus achieved for them a third distinct axis on which to stand and traverse, this time a world of monochromatic green.

Storper, foolishly, faced himself to the left rather than to the right as he rammed the ground and pivoted into it, resulting in him being stuck on the underside of their plane, walking around upside-down, as it were, but still following well enough on account of the substance of this world's surface being translucent and of infinitesimal thickness. This was driving everyone nuts, though, so Dweetle stomped a hole through their shared surface at the exact spot he observed the bottoms of a pair of large, white K-Swiss shoes, sending

Mullignoc falling exactly halfway through before the local gravity caught up with his inverted body. Storper clambered out, all in a tizzy.

"What's the matter, Storps, old boy? It's like you don't know which way is up!" squawked Boovvariun with a wheezy laugh. Dweezle cringed. Carpentrius only rolled his eyes, and then spoke.

"Welcome, sweet children, to the Z-Axis Realm, the only world of its kind. 'The Blithers of Drombulus,' the locals call it."

Unable to warm himself to the idea of locals, Palestriniac continued: "Are we even in the universe anymore?"

What a Dink sort of question, thought Vleffix snarkily. Until Dink spoke up, out-Dinking all.

"*Our* universe?"

"As if that distinction would even make a difference!" snorted Dweetle. "Actually, we haven't even left Daphnis."

"*Yet*," added Quirff with an air of self-satisfied importance. She shot a knowing glance to Carpentrius and gave a wink.

"Is something in your eye, you wannabe tin man?"

The forger's scalding remark shut her up—though she had spoken only a single word, that one adverbial appendation beginning with our beloved alphabet's penultimate letter. In a nervous, rather automatic fashion, Quirff extracted a re-tractable ruby-tipped object from her aluminum faux-scalp, sniffed the tip deeply, and suddenly gave it a lick.

"Whoa. Is that drugs?"

"Storper, even in death, you're *so* dumb," sighed Boov.

"And whatever you were trying to say wasn't even grammatically correct. That's quite obviously android chapstick."

"No it's not!" blurted Dink rudely. "It's—*hahgh!*—it's a *Push Pop!*" He tumbled and tripped over his words in choking laughter, his voice finally cracking on the last two words spoken and exploding into uncontrollable hooting cackles in a shuddering falsetto as tears ran down his face.

This made Mullignoc feel ashamed of his own stupidity, Palestriniac mortified by his own idiocy, and Vleffix frozen with an unfathomable sense of her own unconscionable puerility: a triple whammy that left Carpentrius in a squat, hands on his knees to stabilize himself as he threw his head back in a series of hearty guffaws; and Dweetle, too, lost himself in snorts of laughter that threw him to the ground, and he thrashed about on the faintly glowing translucent green surface.

It was at this point, joining Hodezemiah on the ground, they all lay down and took a nap, for the truth of it was that every last one of them was in a state of delirium brought on by exhaustion. And Dink Flapple hadn't even been able to receive nutrition since Thursday.

CHAPTER 11

Rhombus Jones, the maniac with the mathematic face

Whose badinage unyielding has destroyed the human race,

Was not to be outdone by mystic Magnus MacMortartar

Who, nathless, be the man among the two who strove the

  harder.

—*Dymn Recember,* Sleuth Paste

B AWDY churl!"

"Huh?" Dink had awoken, bleary-eyed and sluggish, but was nonetheless nonplussed by such an indignity, and from Carpentrius, no less.

"Shoddy burl!"

"Uh . . . I don't even—"

"I'd own tea, Vinny. Steven he, dough and leaves Steves."

"—Wait a minute."

"Mate to win it! Weighed the tome, innit?"

"Has Jeptunianizer left you, shell-man?" Flapple shook off

the sleep and grew more alert. He looked up into a pair of inscrutable eyes.

"Your finest dinest fines winer. Swine klein. Clean lines. Shall? Guess nine, yes what. Watermelon eights the listless seedlessness, lest Dresden duresses. Wast whilst whistle still, sis, tell."

"Oh *no*."

Everyone was awake now and staring at the once again unintegrated fibersmith-forger, who beamed winsomely. His splendid smile put Clark Gable's to absolute shame.

"Own *hoe*."

Storper stomped, hoping to be heard by Jeptunianizer the Man within Earth's mantle, but having died, he had forgotten he wasn't even on a planet, much less Earth. He stared down at his feet, un-shoed and -socked again from the former tizzy and still shiny, in fact, from the chili dogs. But this seemed to have excited the shell-man, who stomped and stamped about playfully. (It was a good thing that he, unlike Dweetle, wore something other than studded steel-toe boots.)

"He's worse than ever. Let's ditch him," murmured Quirff under her breath.

The dream team made a run for it, but halfheartedly, because they all soon realized that there was absolutely nowhere to run *to*, as the infinitude of the green emptiness stretched in every direction.

"Hey, it's okay!" said Boovvariun, as a crooked smile of relief crept onto his face. They all saw why it was okay when they looked back to see the unactualized Carpentrius doing pushups.

"What the heck are we even supposed to do, though?" said Dweetle, most uncharacteristically.

"I don't *know!*" cried Vleffix, as if this was a personal affront. "You tell me. You, with your 'riddle of Saturn's rings' omniscience."

"You're one to speak! You abducted Flapple with more purpose than—than purpose itself!"

"That makes *no* sense. *You* make no sense. You've *never* made sense. What a pathetic excuse for a man you are, O Hodezemiah. Using those baggy thug jeans to offset your professorial dorkiness with such self-conscious irony—all without an ounce of hipster dandiness. You know, you make me *sick.*" Quirff proceeded to finish her Push Pop at this point.

"And how do you expect the poor fellow to receive sustenance," continued Dweetle obliviously, looking off and shaking his head, "to say nothing of proper nutrition, with a stomach and digestive tract no longer able to absorb what it ought?"

She twitched. "What makes you say that?"

He leveled his gaze on her. "I know you are to blame, Vleffix. 'Twas Carpentrius who let me see into your mind"— he squinted—"and Dink's."

She steamed. But the expression she wore was one of annoyance, or even impatience, rather than defensiveness.

"Well, well, well," drawled Dink, raising separate eyebrows alternately. "Seems that you more than just *saw* me chug that battery acid the other morning."

"Fine. Fine! I lured your shiftless brother, Nerk, with a simple flutter of my magnetic eyelashes, and before he knew what hit him, he rode his moped right out of my body shop, ready, and most willing, to deliver the goods." She shook her head sardonically, rolling her eyes and smacking her lips.

"So wait. How does that explain anything at all?" remarked Palestriniac, who, along with Mullignoc, had nothing better to do than tune into the admittedly intriguing conversation.

"Well, the leaky car battery was stowed in his moped's handlebar basket—Nerk didn't even notice that his bespattered front tire was already corroded down to the rim when he set off!—and he pulled right up to Dink's prefab bungalow, cawed the family call, and summoned his brother with ease. I'm not even sure any words were exchanged; they shared in 'raise the roof' gesticulations, and before I knew it, Dink was guzzling the battery's contents right out of its 'plus' sign. Hah! I was hiding behind an oak tree and saw it all."

"I was wondering why that old oak was smoldering! *And why it reeked of burnt rubber!*' Dink's eyes bulged maniacally.

"But why?" cried Dweetle, rightfully ignoring Flapple's pointless remark. "Why castrate the boy's digestive processes in such a manner?"

"Yeah!" barked Mullignoc. "I was trying to ask him about how he didn't get sick from the Soviet nuclear tomato sauce, you know, back when we met the forger, and now I know, I guess . . . but is my soul brother *starving*, then?"

"Can't you see?" Vleffix squinted caustically. "Had I not, I could never have tested his bravery and resolve in my '93 Taurus." Dink squinted now too, and flexed, but she continued: "It's true that I was less aware than you, Dweetle, of the full extent of the consequences of battery acid ingestion, what with the esophageal cauterization and all, but it was just as well since it was my intention to put him into anaphylactic shock anyway—again, to test his mettle. You see, he thought the peanutty candy bar I compelled him to ingest—"

"—*half*-bar—"

"—was the last hurrah, his being forced to stare death right in the face. And—"

"—*half*-death—"

"Shut up. I'm trying to talk about how brave you are." She turned back to the others. "And he really is brave, if exasperating; noble, if barbaric. And the best part is, all this is but preparation for what is to come."

"Yep, not surprised. Right? Or *am* I?" He bit his lip and wrinkled his nose to look awesome, nodding slightly.

"Uh, what are you trying to ask?" She paused briefly. "You don't even know, do you?" Dink kissed his bicep. She winced, quickly looking away toward the others. "But the fact that he is slowly starving to death is entirely inconsequential to the kamikaze mission for which he has signed up."

"'Signed up'?" spluttered Boov indignantly.

"Well, yes, on the subconscious level, at least."

"I never even realized how ready I am to fake the faking of my own death," nodded Dink distantly.

But Hodezemiah Dweetle was in a cold sweat and shaking his jowls like an old hound dog: "The cavy's got my wallet chain!"

CHAPTER 12

Vork Stippensi, infamous shrimp-breeder, he
Preferred the prime prawns of the Caspian Sea
But his partner, Snoot Butterick, laughingly lauded
Moist oysters that, when pre-ingested, applauded!

—*Dilbeus Phrantic,* Torn Sea Sponges

S URE enough, Klaus was loose yet again and tugging at Dweetle with his little mouth, which was already crowded with (as it happened) several strands of carbon fiber. It was as if the dear blob of fur was trying to get the rotund little man's attention.

"Wait a minute! What's that you've got, young sir?" The carbon fiber clenched in the guinea pig's jaws distracted the bearer of the wallet chain to such a degree that his shakes had already subsided, and Dweetle stooped down to remove the mouth-items.

"Wait, has he *swallowed* a part of that?" asked Dink in a half-whisper, hurriedly taking Hodez's place. Sure enough, the strands merged at the back of Klaus's mouth, and as

Flapple gingerly extracted it, bits turned to inches, and inches to yards. Klaus kept his mouth open obligingly, and eleven minutes or so later, our main man had removed some three hundred feet of thin cable, now coiled neatly by Palestriniac, terminating in an electrical plug of three prongs. Klaus gagged a little bit at the end, understandably, and Quirff released her held breath as soon as she realized that the rodent retching would not be productive after all.

She then widened her eyes and gasped. Quickly looking at everyone in turn, she grabbed the plug and shrieked "Shell-man!"

No sooner had she grabbed the plug than the other loose end rose up and started getting sucked into nothingness, as if falling sideways through an invisible drain suspended in midair. Quirff struggled against the ticking clock to reach Carpentrius (now on his twenty-seventh set of one hundred pushups and very much in the zone) and, once she succeeded in doing so, located an outlet on the bottom of his left foot and connected the plug, taking care to wrap some excess cable around his left ankle several times. As the cable continued to retract, the forger was pulled off his feet and dragged several feet, then pulled high into the air with the last bit of cable—only to get stuck there, dangling upside-down and growing increasingly translucent and immaterial.

A man dressed in bluejeans alone fell from the darkness above, directly above the shell-man, in fact, until they were occupying precisely the same physical space in the universe, at which time the cable was immediately loosed and sucked into nothingness. Carpentrius, re-Jeptunianized, fell to the ground with a tidy judo-tumble, once again in his bicycle shorts and polo shirt.

"Where do the jeans go?" whispered Mullignoc.

"They're a part of his soul, no doubt" returned Palestriniac simply.

Flapple couldn't believe how satisfactory a reply that was and playfully chucked his wigged friend once he had him in a secure enough headlock.

"Yeah!" hollered Dink.

"Calm down, you two. Yours truly—well, my Jeptunianizer self—has been busy rendering *this.*" Carpentrius held aloft what looked for all the world like a packet of fast-food soy sauce.

"Yeah!" shouted Storper.

"Stop talking," hissed Vleffix. She wore an expression of outright hunger as she eyed the packet.

Carpentrius stroked his mustache and, for the first time in a very long while, lit up his pipe. He produced a folding stool and took a seat. After a languid puff or two, he met a few eyes and said: "Gravity Grease."

Dweetle pursed his lips with expectancy. Quirff grunted involuntarily, which made her blush.

* * *

Quirff Johnson was born a little outside of Cleveland to parents Phil and Jeanine, both of whom practiced ventriloquism on a professional, competitive level. Though she swore "Vleffix" to be her given name, it was not: "Wilhelmina Winifred

Johnson" was the name that appeared on her birth certificate, and it was by design that her parents named her such in order to call her "Minnie Winnie." It was her frustration with being two heads taller than all the boys while being a "Minnie" that she resolved, upon adulthood, to legally change her name to "Vleffix," after the heroine from her favorite TV movie, *The Infernal Steel Princess of the Stainless Robot Men.* She was, however, awkwardly mistaken about the name of the robot-ruling femme fatale, who was actually called Lil Vefficks; she was addressed "Vil Lefficks" but once, halfway through the movie, and that by the love interest, Gerald, who had a tendency to speak in spoonerisms.

But oh, how Minnie Winnie latched onto that one incorrect pronunciation of the name, and as a little girl not yet in the habit of eliding consecutive consonant sounds (instead, creating the unnecessary but popular *schwa* between them), one can see how the syllables "Vil Leff–" would be counted as one and the same as "Vleff"—yes, in the mind's ear of a young child; to say nothing, nothing at all, of "icks" and "ix," which are, of course, nothing less than utterly homophonous. And even had she wanted to, Vleffix would never have been able to fact-check herself later in life anyway, as the execrable movie never again aired, and as no trace of *The Infernal Steel Princess,* nor any reference to it, exists; one would need outright omniscience to call her out on her error.

Being tall, her parents, friends, and pastor pressured her into playing basketball, and it was her YMCA teammates who affectionately dubbed her "Quirff" after, in a reverie, she had said to her inner circle, "Doesn't the dribble of the ball with its accompanying gym-reverberation make the most beautiful *quirff* sound?" She embraced the name, as it preserved the double-F spelling of her other made-up name, the one that, by the age of eighteen, had indeed become her legal moniker.

At 25, she had made Carpentrius's acquaintance at a job fair for machinists, and ultimately it was he who convinced her, when she shattered her tibia, to replace her entire leg with his own bit of combustion-driven electrobionic phantasmagadgetry rather than receive the traditional and very routine orthopedic surgery. With "Lêg_2.0" came the promise of geomagical skills and further protochemical, metavoltaic powers, which she knew she couldn't pass up. And so the Rhapsodic Council began.

* * *

"But I could've sworn that gravity itself was kinda greasy already," complained Dink.

Palestriniac and Mullignoc cackled slyly, pretending to agree, though self-conscious in their inability to actually understand: a poignant irony, as all they would actually have needed to understand was that there *was* nothing to actually understand.

"What indeed, sir, are its applications and uses—this Gravity Grease?" asked Dweetle, pushing his glasses back on his nose.

"I think I know!" shrieked Quirff like a giddy schoolgirl. "Can I venture a guess?"

"Your venture would be a *Chevy* Venture, no doubt—judging by your taste in cars, and self-respect," asserted the smith-forger extraordinaire.

"'Her *taste* in *self-respect*'?" asked Dink quizzically (though unable to refrain from smiling hugely).

"And I'm sure it tastes awful," quipped Carpentrius, looking down at the pipe he was packing once again. He proceeded to cross his legs above the knee, as self-assured gents do.

Leaving Dink dumbfounded and Quirff with tears in her eyes, he continued. "It's what you might guess, and I'm sure what Quirffy was going to say: Apply it wherever you want a local, customizable source of gravity. One little squirt gives you something like a modest magnetic attraction, or static cling, while the whole pack gives you enough force to override the naturally occurring gravity of entire nations of people."

"A city-state of space-time!"

"Whose curvature brings on the rhyme!"

"As well, Einsteinian gravitas!"

"All in a pack of special sauce!"

Boovvariun had made the first remark, Dink the second, Hodezemiah the third, and Storper, of course, the fourth. Carpentrius slowly shook his head, grinning, so impressed was he. He gave everyone high-fives in turn; the atmosphere, by the powerful impression left by the poetic feat, was hushed. Vleffix had not contributed because she was moping on account of the forger's previous words, although she did hold out her hand to slap him some skin—only to be denied.

That same denier spoke once more: "Oh, how I could use

Blastula and the butler right about now." Blastula Harbig-ginotham, the gruff receptionist heretofore mentioned only once, stood in wait, even now, in the secret palace-cave beneath the Indian Ocean isle of Badrad Baldi. She would be waiting a while yet. The butler, he and all his koans sorely missed by Carpentrius, was on Earth as well, lost in existential thought about the nonexistence of thoughts unthought.

"She had a knack for bearing news of all kinds with nonchalance," he continued, "and he kept me on my toes with his wonderful, stupid lines of questioning."

"Why speak of them in the past tense?" stammered Dweetle.

"Ah! Now that's a good question. It's because they're dead —well, at least from where we're standing."

"Axis Z?" tried Dink.

"Right you are; as, indeed, all humanity is long dead, again, in terms of the conscious experience peculiar to this third axis of being."

"That being the z-axis?" gasped Storper.

"And none other," answered Carpentrius patiently.

"I just *said* that!" hissed Dink in Mullignoc's ear, delivering a rough elbow-jab to the ribs. The dead one winced. Boov burst out laughing. His wig was such a mess by now.

"Yes, these Blithers of Drombulus do have a way of rendering us all *Storperized!*" remarked Palestriniac with an insufferably ingratiating air.

The forger and Flapple, together, looked down their noses at him. The former's own powers of idiot-detection were as fine-tuned as they were famous, and they (complete with accompanying body language) must have been rubbing off on the latter, flawed and dumpsome though he was.

"You're no local," shot Vleffix. "How dare you call it that." Dweetle couldn't help but agree and sneered accordingly.

"I'm afraid you are mistaken: Among our little party, Storper Mullignoc remains unmatched in his deceasedness," said Carpentrius, now smiling wryly. "As for the rest of us here, it is not we who are dead, only everyone else."

"But how is it that everyone else is dead? Can you really reduce the ultimate reality of another's life or death to one's own interdimensional mode of experience?" pressed Hodezemiah.

"In this realm, you bet your buns you can."

"But you haven't answered anything, Carpentrius!"

"And *you* never even asked why I said I could really use my receptionist and butler right about now, you old philosopher."

"But I thought you already—you don't even—I mean, who cares if—" Dweetle rolled his eyes and issued a small growl between clenched teeth: "Aaagh! Okay: why, *why?*"

"Because I could use the pick-me-up of their loving company." He winked. "But yes, they're dead. I couldn't tell you why, or how. All I know is, every time I'm in these parts, I invariably receive word from my robotic sources that everyone's died off, only to find them all alive again when I return. I had doubts about my robots' reliability at first, of course, but after several optical refiberings and carbonic recalibrations, the results remained the same, always."

CHAPTER 13

*Implausible, nay impossible, imposable improbably im-
passable posies non-disposable irascible indefensibly inde-
fatigable but ostensibly tensely imploding free-radical-
promoting fossils denoting apostles in my nostrils.*

—Blauvgner Gnaughftspryst, My Ankle

B OOV looked up at the forger all of a sudden: "Wait.
Does Storp's being dead have to do with this?"
"Nope."
"Let's not talk in circles, now," warned Dweetle. "His
Grace still has much to discuss, I'm sure. He's been saying so
since those dangerous chili dogs"—he glared—"even though
he has yet to actually spit it out."
"Hodezemiah Dodecadog Dweetle! I've had just about
enough of the bellicose manner, and I'm sure our fiber optic
superman could say the same," lectured Quirff.
Dweetle turned bright red at the mention of his middle
name, given to him in honor of the singular name his parents'
used for their three pet dogs, which were always kept bound

together, side by side, with soft but strong woven silk ribbons. (Before the dogs passed, Mr. and Mrs. Dweetle would install young Hodez atop Dodecadog in a waterskier's stance, via foot clamps integrated into the two woven junctions between the three dogs.) But it was Carpentrius who provided the reply to the admonition of our machine woman.

"Don't speak for me, servant. And had I any such words to speak, which I don't, they would be far less clicky on account of my conspicuous lack of ill-fitting wooden dentures."

It was Quirff's turn to blush once again. Poor Quirff. She whipped out a PayDay to eat through her sorrows. She was as worthy of such self-pity as she was deserving of its consolation prize: quite. The peanut-heavy candy bar proved the perfect drug.

Dink, however, had different notions of drugs and perfection both. (After all, he was, as you well know, kind reader, an absurd metaphysical specimen of a man.) Having nonchalantly popped open the packet on one end, he took a sucking swig of none other than that fearsome Gravity Grease, finishing it off like nothing.

Carpentrius, stunned for once, impulsively patted his pockets (though his shorts had none) and looked around wildly, then, at Dweetle, searchingly. But Hodezemiah, mid-shrug, had already slid sideways through the air and fallen to Flapple, and so had all the others. The forger, in cartoon fashion, joined in the moment he realized that he, too, must obey the laws of nature (newly-profaned though they may be). They all found their footing and stood upon the surface of the still-upright Dink Bucephalus Flapple II, each of them jutting out in different directions, each like a hair standing on end.

"WHOA! WHICH WAY IS UP?" screamed Palestriniac, stumbling around on Flapple's left kneepit.

"AND WHICH WAY IS DOWN?" shouted Storper Mullignoc, windmilling both arms frantically as the bottoms of his slippery feet swiveled about from the outside to the frontside of Dink's right thigh.

"*EVERY* WAY IS DOWN!" screeched Flapple, who was having trouble keeping his extremities from buckling under the gravitational force of his own trunk, though keeping his knees and elbows unbent and his limbs extended seemed to help a bit.

"I don't know about this," said Quirff, standing atop the right side of Dink's face, nervously shifting from one foot to the other.

"Well, I do," said Dweetle, deep in thought, hands in his pockets, alternately leaning back on his heels and rolling his feet forward again across the back of Dink's neck.

"Praytell," whispered Carpentrius, balanced on one leg on the outside of Flapple's left buttock, holding the other aloft.

Suddenly, a big chunk of ice from outer space pelted Dweetle in the gut.

Indeed, outer space. What had happened was this. Axes Z and Y, being (thanks to the locals) elusive spatial planes of existence and, therefore, reluctant to manifest to outsiders in the first place, no longer had any hold on our adventurers once the Gravity Grease was loosed in such reckless quantities. As such, these ultra-exotic realms appeared to collapse before their very eyes, leaving them in the bland dust of dumb old Daphnis, with its tiresomely spectacular view of Saturn's rings.

But you see, it was the Saturnian moon that had fallen to the bottoms of Dink's feet, and not the other way around—all in an instant.

Again, Hodez had been smacked in the paunch by some space ice. Consequently, he fell bodily to Flapple, ending up in the fetal position, on his side, having landed on Dink's upper back just between his shoulders.

(Dink was just crawling with people, but also Klaus, who circumambulated his lower trunk by way of a trans-abdominal scurry to the left love handle, lower back, right love handle, abdomen again, and so on.)

Boovvariun was hungry, so he took a ripe, rather spotted banana out of his inside vest pocket, split open the peel at the stem, and began to eat. The final bite's worth suddenly came loose and fell out of the peel. He nearly dropped it but caught it and sighed with relief, but must have sighed too hard, be-cause he relaxed too much and dropped it after all. Dweetle, still in the fetal position, attempted to recover it only to bat at it a little bit, knocking it in a slightly new direction. Dink turned his head to see what was going on on his upper back, and the banana bite fell into his mouth. He chewed and ate, quite unfazed.

Palestriniac discarded the banana peel by tossing it over his shoulder, and it fell onto Dink's right cheek, that is to say, at Vleffix's feet. Disgusted, she kicked it away, but it just fell back to her, landing right on top of her feet this time. She removed her detachable leg and flung the peel so forcefully that it went into orbit around Dink's person.

Flapple, whose thinking was growing more disordered all the time, suddenly exclaimed, "I can't believe Quirff is an elderly bald man! Look! That doesn't even *look* like her!"

"That's not *me*! That's not even a person's head; it's Storper's kneecap, you twit! How is it you're not aware I'm standing on the side of your face?"

"Because I can't even *see* you!"

She fumed. "But you were just—! What am I supposed to even—!"

"Spit it out, you Kurt Vonnegut fever dream!"

"Oh Carpentrius!" interjected Boovvariun. "I was hoping you would say something!"

"And why, Mr. Palestriniac, were you hoping for such a thing as that?"

"Well sir, I think it's safe to say we're all wondering what will become of us now. . . ."

"Nothing other than what was meant to happen all along, only much sooner than anyone could have anticipated: Dink must—"

But he was interrupted by Dink imploding. His head and limbs fell into his torso, which compressed itself into a fleshy sphere. Everyone stumbled about to find new footing, but their bones were getting crushed instantaneously, and, faster still, their bodies were being pulverized by Dink's super-gravity's compressive process, which rendered them all, at a speed much faster than light, a zero-dimensional singularity that turned itself inside-out in a manner defying time and space, leaving everyone gasping for breath as their now-unannihilated selves traversed the Einstein-Rosen Bridge conjured by the black hole that was Dink. Yes, our boy had accomplished what Carpentrius had historically sought to avoid in his own travels: arrival prior to departure. Ah! but whither?

"WHOA!" shouted Dink.

Everyone screamed all the louder in reply to the man who had become a wormhole that had become a man again.

"I feel like a man again!" shouted Dink.

"You stole my line, you old cad, you!" chuckled Carpentrius. Everybody applauded.

CHAPTER 14

The bungular jungles of Spitzian Splasm—
Immensely immaculate, chaotic chasm—
Grew jolly and jangled, angled, though spangled
With fruits of fruitopian bounty.
The briniest branches brodiddled sweet plantches
As pants of particular practical ranches
Dressed up in their dressing, as messes not messing
With any Európean county.

—Skinndivvius Grinne, Manicdotes (1911 edition)

B UT everything after the "WHOA!" was in Dink's head, I suppose, for he stood alone in the middle of the street on his own neighborhood block. He performed a quick guinea pig check and after not finding Klaus in his fanny pack, checked his beanie and found the magnificent rodent sweetly snoring just inside it. He replaced his beanie and shook his head with a little sigh of affection. *Klaus, oh Klaus, my son, with your flowing coat of fur,* he thought verblessly.

Just then he caught sight of a dubious lad unicycling with headphones on, and dark sunglasses for good measure, in the direction of a 1993 Ford Taurus. Dink ran at the speeding car and jumped onto it, shattering its windshield. Brakes screeched as it drifted and fishtailed, and as it came to rest sideways on the street, out jumped Vleffix. Dink was flung preposterously, but landed okay. The unicyclist passed by with a gentle swerve.

"Get in the car."

Dink got up. "Wait . . . *what?* But I thought—"

"GET IN THE CAR."

He started to obey. But paused.

". . . No."

Steam was rising off the tips of each one of her 10,000 skullcap hair-wires, and she was shaking with fresh rage, but both of them were distracted just then by a retching noise just half a block beyond the wrecked car. They tore their eyes off of each other to take a look.

They saw the unicyclist (nauseated, surely, by the close call) projectile-vomiting onto a fire hydrant, which exploded. He kept riding.

Vleffix stared after him, terrified, then stared at the unicycle champ beside her, and then stared at the other one again, who was now vanishing in the distance, and stammered, "Th-that battery acid puke was for my car though."

Dink stared, too, but with bewilderment rather than terror, and when he tried, after staring at the other champ, to stare at himself, his eyes only crossed. He shook it off, and his eyes righted themselves.

"Quirff! I thought by saving my own life you'd leave well enough alone. But here you are, bossing me around again. Yeah, so—" He stopped short, looked around, and put his hands in his pockets. "So what's up?" Now he was trying to look all casual and cool. (Had he a collar like Carpentrius did, he definitely would have popped it. He still wore his hot pink long sleeved tee, though, so he just pantomimed the collar-popping.)

"'What's up'?" She trembled. "*What's up?* You time-traveled, Dink Flapple, I can see that now, and now the original you didn't burn a hole through the floorboard of my car, and now I simply don't know what to do to get the necessary chain of events to ensue. And why you traveled back from the future only to burn the bridge that got you to that future in the first place is beyond me. All I know is, I fear for the futures of everyone involved. I mean, how are you still here? You just now kept your upcoming trip back in time from happening."

"But I couldn't have kept it from happening just now, because then I never would have been able to end up here to keep it from happening."

"Yes, it's the classic time-travel paradox you see in all those movies. So cliché. But chilling nonetheless, especially since it is now our reality."

"Hey, how did you figure all that out so quickly anyway?"

"Figure what out?"

"That I traveled in time, and that I came from the future."

Quirff shivered as if cold. "Well, I didn't at first. After initially thinking the unicyclist was you, I saw you jump on my car and knew *that* was you, not on your vehicle, for some reason, and I thought that maybe you were trying to keep a fellow cyclist safe—or something; I don't know. (But then, why did you jump on my car instead of simply shoving your unicycling self out of harm's way, you idiot? See, it's so *confusing*.) Anyway, it was only when I saw the caustic, explosive vomiting that I realized that *that* was you too, and that the you I'm now talking to must have been in the know and, therefore, from the future.

"Goll, Quirff. You've gotta be the smartest piece of bio-technology I've ever met."

"Did you just call me a *piece*?" She gave him a wholehearted shove, and it was then that she noticed the words on his shirt were backward, as in a mirror. (The shirt should have read: JACK KEROUAC'S FLAPJACK SHACK.) *A grotesque side-effect of time travel, no doubt,* she thought. Pictured, also, were some pancakes, which really didn't look much different in reverse, and Kerouac himself, on the road, but the left side, giving the syrupy food a ride in a 1949 Hudson Commodore, whose steering wheel was, quite obviously at this point, on the right. Flapple noticed Vleffix staring at his shirt, which made him look down at it.

"Heh, what a backward beatnik! How contra-counter-cultural! A real rebel in retrograde!"

Hodezemiah chuckled.

Why yes, sweet reader, Hodezemiah Dweetle it was. They both turned to see him coming out of the trunk of Quirff's car. She gasped, then scoffed.

"Dweetle! You wily turd, where did you come from?"

"The same place I did, you campy robot woman from the end of *Superman III*," sneered Carpentrius, fibersmith-forger. "Out of the trunk of your Jurassic-Park-era Ford, of course."

"Oh, Carpentrius! You're here!" she beamed, then took a deep breath. "How I adore the indomitable man you are, and although it's been years"—she became choked up—"ah, even so, how your gibes wear on me!"

"And Boov wears a *wig* on him!" snorted Storper, who was cracking himself up even before the witless statement had fully exited his mouth. He had come out from behind some hydrangea bushes near the fire hydrant, which he had blown up with the free sample packet of Drano that had been stowed in the fifth pocket of his Lee jean shorts. Already dead, he was unharmed.

Palestriniac, riding back on the unicycle and sporting headphones and shades recently lifted from an unsuspecting summer school, tipped his head in acknowledgment, which allowed his headphones to fall around his neck, making way for the wig, which he quickly replaced as though formerly naked. Tossing an empty bottle of ipecac over his shoulder onto someone's lawn, he dismounted neatly beside the car's back bumper, on which Dweetle's baggy jeans were caught, though their owner had wriggled free of them since he knew he was wearing some Umbro shorts underneath anyway.

Quirff and Dink gaped, stunned, at Carpentrius.

"Oh yes. Tricked you both." He stood there winsomely and lovelily, not even needing to pop his collar.

"*Am* I a time traveler or not?" Dink started to cry.

"Oh, my boy, my boy! You most certainly are! We all

are, only you arrived having fallen asleep standing up, so I took the opportunity to stage an elaborate prank. Yes, dear boy, we are *all* time travelers, except for Vleffix—that is, *that* Vleffix there. But *this* one—"

Just then, Vleffix climbed out of the trunk of her own car. "What is it you were saying about the third *Superman* movie?"

"That it's the worst, like you," quipped the forger.

The Quirffs looked at each other and burst into tears.

Carpentrius walked over to the one who didn't come out of the trunk and patted her on the shoulder. "All the rest of us are from the future," he murmured warmly, "so I'd really love it if you would go away." She gave a sob. "And take that unremarkable sedan of yours with you."

She was about to lose it completely when she noticed her windshield had somehow been mended perfectly, with the speed and precision of fiber optics themselves. She met eyes with the forger and he gave her a wink.

"Oh, and you can hit Dink with your car a little bit later today, I promise." He winked again, and then, using his pipe, flashed the signal indicating to Boovvariun that it was time to sneak Dink's unicycle back into his carport. Boov missed it.

She wiped her eyes and grinned a small, wooden grin. Then she returned to her car and drove off.

And just like that, Dweetle's pants were gone.

CHAPTER 15

He enjoyed the food that his mouth chewed,

And how well did that mouth of his chew for him!

The teeth of his mouth were the chewers themselves,

Though the jaws were the openers and closers of them;

The jaws of none other than he who enjoyed

All that food that he chewed with the mouth he employed

That did chewing so well for that very same man

Whose own chewing, though ensuing 'thout pretext or plan,

Simply couldn't occur without teeth that defer

The real action of chewing to the jaws and their doing.

But was it merely a means to an end: to enjoyment

Brought on by his tongue's gustatorial employment?

—*Wrage Buke-Hannon,* Bland Miracles

I T was the remaining Quirff's turn to be comforted as she said to Carpentrius, "How your jibes wear on me!"

The pantsless Dweetle shot her a glance. "You just said that."

"The *other* you," added Palestriniac.

"Hey, that's right! Verbatim!" said Mullignoc, trying to appear far more intelligent than he was, which didn't work since the final word spoken was enunciated rather conspicuously and with far too hard a 't.'

"Very nearly," corrected the forger, "but 'gibes' was used first, not 'jibes.' Or at least that's what my dear butler would say."

But nobody there could read what he had just said, so without bothering to wait for a reaction that could never come, Carpentrius continued.

"But I just tease you so because I *love* you, old girl. I am proud of every last one of you, you know. We did this together, and we didn't even have to brave the infamous Muds of Squonk.[3] No soul could have anticipated the elegance of our solution!" He looked around, shining his face upon them.

"Solution?" repeated Dink.

The forger puffed his pipe thoughtfully, and said, "Our solution to the riddle of Saturn's rings, and nothing less."

"But first, what is the riddle itself?" queried Palestriniac.

And with that, Dweetle intoned:

> *This is the cycle of mine, like the moon's*
>
> *Though the cycle, recycled, is like a bassoon's:*
>
> *Ringing about but with low frequency,*
>
> *Or rather, with singular plane, like the sea;*
>
> *A cycle of oneness, if made up by many*
>
> *Fine rings that, alone, be considered too skinny*
>
> *For purposes higher than mere revolution;*

Evolving revolving begets the solution.

The singular cycle, the cycle of one:

It is this that I am when especially spun.

"A unicycle!" cried Dink.

"You *would* think that," scoffed Vleffix.

"No, but . . . but I think he's right!" said Hodezemiah brightly.

"The solution is a—a unicycle?" asked Storper skeptically, looking up from the ground.

"'Evolving revolving begets the solution,'" repeated Boovvariun thoughtfully. "So . . . Dink's own work on the uni has evolved, even revolutionized, the sport."

"Huh?" squinted Vleffix. "Why are you bringing Dink into the riddle?"

"Because it was he," interjected Carpentrius, "who scaled the face of the Burj Khalifa without dismounting his unicycle even once. Because it was he, and he alone, who dared to cross the Bering Strait on the surface of the frigid Arctic waters, even though it proved a spectacular failure. Because it was he who duct-taped the torn space suit he wore, hopped back onto his trusty vehicle, and proceeded, off-camera, to outpace the moon rover on the 100-mile trek back to the module. He is the embodiment, the very personification, of the great one-wheeled beauty."

"Dink begets the solution!" announced Boov triumphantly.

Dweetle continued: "And Dink, while a black hole, begat a hyperspatial portal to the past—"

"—thereby ushering in a new era," interrupted the forger,

"the era of time travel, time travel for the everyman, which will continue through the harvesting of raw materials on Daphnis, the refining of them into Gravity Grease by fiber-smith-forging inside Earth's mantle, and—we only know this last part thanks to you, Dink Flapple—the ingestion of an entire packet of Grease by a recklessly fun-loving individual."

"But . . . humanity will need to get out to Saturn every time, then. That might not be so easy; we don't all have chalkdust and magic mirrors," muttered Quirff.

"Hey," said the forger in a hushed voice, smirking coyly. "Look up."

And everyone obeyed Carpentrius. There, hanging in the sky just above the treetops, quite visible in the full daylight, was a goofy little lump of a moon. Daphnis.

Flapple sensed something in his periphery and, startled, found Carpentrius looking right at him.

"Dink."

"Yes, Sir Carpentrius?"

"That was you. Your gravity brought that moon here, baby."

They high-fived.

"And hey, how's your stomach lining? Still cauterized?"

"No, I think it's all better. I think the black hole thing kicked it."

They high-fived again, even harder.

EPILOGUE

XXVIII: OF BINOCULARS UNHINGED.

Seismic McSleaze, Mars's first protobadger
Had bigged the Earth's only small-eyed weaselcatcher.
Prone to be bested but never outbigged
(The bestment of having had Newtons de-Figged),
Ol' Smalleye summarily did gadget the gadger.

"Not with a 'G' but a 'B,' don't you see,"
The badger-prote just now reminded just me.
But, barding it best, 'tis on 'G' I insist,
And "gadger" it stays, though the 'B' will be missed.
And the trapper of weasels just then slapped his knee!

"I am not just a catcher," said he, "but a doctor
Of eyes of small size, and I fly helicopter."
"Just one?" quipped the poet. "The plural's a given:
A pilot can pilot a singular, riven."
"One 'copter I pilot, but two eyes I doctor."

And wryly he smirked, the old quack of a weaseler,
As if measles could possibly be any measler.
McSleaze then replied, as if out of the blue,
"I'll love you forever, you old joker, you!"
Thus the joculest oculist unbigged the Sleazler.

EPILOGUE II

THEY gathered, one and all—time-traveling heroes stuck in their own recent past—around Palestriniac and Mullignoc's cathode ray tube television set, as it had not yet been destroyed by the westward asphalt torrent effected by Quirff's perturbless will. Boov hopped up, surprisingly spryly, to switch the knob from UHF to VHF for the network premiere of the first episode of *Scissors Scandals: The Final Season*.

Being the absurd maniac he was, Jovantrick Spatchel's nemesis, Rapscaldric the Invincible, had once again hijacked a food truck, but this time, one used for sweet rather than savory fare. Yes, it was Rhythe Splamdectric's Spectacular 'Lectric Fudgemobile that had had fallen victim to the Invincible this time.

Having suddenly jumped out of a less-used cupboard, Rapscaldric high-kicked the small team of chocolatiers clear through the custom skylights, which rained shattered glass all over the cackling villain.

His cutting laughter continued even as he hurried to the wheel to regain control of the vehicle—the driver, Rhythe Splamdectric himself, had perished in the chaos through cocoa powder-induced asphyxiation—as it barreled down the expressway.

But it was too late: Who should he find at the wheel already—and not Rhythe's corpse!—but the Aberrant Abhorrence of the accordio-wigmastering underground himself, the one and only Jovantrick Spatchel, donning his entire stock of contraband wings as makeshift clothing, and rocking out to "The Westphalian Polka," which played through the dashboard's aftermarket cassette deck. The speakers blared lustily.

Out of Rapscaldric's custom-tailored tuxedo's cumberbund's hidden marsupial pocket jumped his superintelligent weasel, Smudge, who quickly clambered into the dashboard and changed the cassette to Side 2; and alas, the live version of the very same polka played.

"Aghh!" shrieked Smudge in legitimately well thought-out exasperation.

Spatchel shook his head to the music groovily, totally unfazed, even as he covertly armed and fired a fudge bullet pop from a canon d'cacao with his left foot. (The Fudgemobile had automatic transmission, and the way the Melodica-Mafia Phenom saw it, that other foot of his was hurting for something to do anyway!) His aim was true, and the Invincible's head exploded.

Rapscardric's body, however, continued trying to wrest control of the steering wheel.

"Ha-HAH! They don't call me the Invincible for nothing!" said his exposed neck hole.

The abovementioned's body tensed with grunting, and a new head sprouted, fully-grown and even more handsome than the original, as he sat right on Jovantrick's lap, causing the vehicle (finally) to crash: It had smashed right through the front doors of a long-vacant 1950s high school building.

"No *way!*" Boovvariun jumped out of his beanbag, assumed a power-squat stance, and pumped his fist uncontrollably.

Conveniently enough for them—but not Smudge, whose guts splattered obscenely—the hero and villain were neatly thrown through the windshield, unimpeded by the by-now-much-discussed dashboard, and landed on their feet upon stark beige linoleum. A heavy drumbeat kicked in, with electric guitars screaming.

Jovantrick didn't even see the bucket of steaming hot fudge Rapscaldric had somehow been holding all along; didn't see it, that is, until its contents were thrown at his face. But then it was the Invincible's turn to be surprised, for Spatchel had simply chugged every last bit of the chocolate splash at a cool 46 miles per hour.

With a twinkle in his eye, and in an unexpectedly playful tone of voice, Jovantrick Spatchel taunted, "If you're so invincible, I challenge you to enclose yourself in a box of your own conjuring that even YOU can't get out of!"

"A logical impossibility!" shot back Rapscaldric.

"What, you're going to let THAT get in your way?"

"... N-no!" he stammered defensively.

He went straight to work, enclosing himself perfectly in an invincible box composed of an impervious material of his own devising. Spatchel clapped his hands together with glee and walked away, a bounce in his step.

The screen faded to black with low, somber piano music, and the credits began to roll—too fast, as always. Then Palestriniac and Mullignoc noticed Palestriniac and Mullignoc pulling up in the driveway in the latter's faded turquoise Geo Metro.

"Whoa, let's get outta here!" they said in unison.

Hodezemiah Dweetle scurried out the back door, and Boov and Storper followed close behind. Quirff and Carpentrius flew away out an open window, but Dink was in the bathroom, whistling.

When, at last, he came out, he noticed his displaced unicycle, which Palestriniac had mistakenly ridden home, on the floor in the entryway. Knowing he had to get it back to his own carport so he could find it, Dink Bucephalus Flapple II hopped on and rode out the front door just as it was thrown open by a living, breathing Storper Mullignoc. He and Boovvariun Palestriniac, hands full of groceries, barely jumped out of the way in time, and all the bags fell, freezer meals spilling everywhere.

END NOTES

1. *"Mitochondrial retractions inchoate,*
   Refracting infraction, splasmic plosives explastic,
   Somnambular dongle blongulous,
   Ingratiating expatriates cheese grating!"
2. Bonck Swignito, Dink Senior's brother-in-law, was, as it happens, the inventor of the first 3-D pince-nez.
3. Along those notorious Squonkic Muds, the indigenous Psytoplaxtrians are cannibals of the worst sort, for after they have hunted down their own kind, they eat them alive. They are able to remain vegan only by virtue of being sentient vegetables themselves.